Lemon the Duck

written by **Laura Backman**

illustrated by **Laurence Cleyet-Merle**

Lobster Press ™

To Richy – my father, my friend, my inspiration. – *Laura Backman*

To my two ducklings, Romane and Maxime. – *Laurence Cleyet-Merle*

Lemon the Duck
Text © 2008 Laura Backman
Illustrations © 2008 Laurence Cleyet-Merle

Published by Lobster Press™
1620 Sherbrooke Street West, Suites C & D
Montréal, Québec   H3H 1C9
Tel. (514) 904-1100 • Fax (514) 904-1101
www.lobsterpress.com

Publisher: Alison Fripp
Editors: Alison Fripp & Meghan Nolan
Editorial Assistants: Lindsay Cornish & Emma Stephen
Graphic Design & Production: Tammy Desnoyers

We acknowledge the financial support of the Government of Canada through the Book Publishing Industry Development Program (BPIDP) for our publishing activities.

We acknowledge the support of the Canada Council for the Arts for our publishing program.

We acknowledge the support of the government of Québec, tax credit for book publishing, administered by SODEC.

Library and Archives Canada Cataloguing in Publication

Backman, Laura
     Lemon the duck / Laura Backman ; Laurence Cleyet-Merle, illustrator.

ISBN 978-1-897073-74-2

     1. Ducks--Juvenile fiction. I. Cleyet-Merle, Laurence II. Title.
PZ10.3.B32Le 2008   j813'.6   C2007-904642-8

Printed and bound in Singapore.

Richard was the first to hear the soft peeping sounds.
Then the rest of the class heard it too. It was coming
from the incubator in Ms. Lake's class.

For twenty-eight days,
the machine had
carefully warmed and
turned four eggs.

Now the children could hear the ducklings peeping inside the eggs, as if to say, "I'm ready to come out!" The students had been studying oviparous animals – egg layers.

The ducklings worked and rested and worked some more until finally, they burst out of the eggs. There lay four ducklings, small and wet, squeaking softly. The children squealed with glee.

Peaches

Lemon

All day, Ms. Lake's students watched in wonder as the four newborns became dry, frisky, peeping balls of fluff. The children named them Peaches, Lemon, Daisy, and Chip-Chip.

Daisy

Chip-Chip

It soon became clear that Lemon, named for her soft yellow down that reminded Ms. Lake of her grandmother's lemon meringue pie, was different. She had a tuft of white on her head, but that wasn't the only thing that set her apart.

"Ms. Lake, what's wrong with Lemon?" Myra asked. "She doesn't stand like the others. She doesn't stretch out her neck."

Ms. Lake called Dr. Bill, the vet.

"Lemon may need a little more time to get her land legs," Dr. Bill said.

Over the next few weeks, the ducklings were fed and loved by
Ms. Lake's class. Soon, white pinfeathers began to poke out of the ducks'
soft down. They were growing up. Little webbed feet slapped against the
floor as the ducklings waddled and flapped and followed the
children around the room. But Lemon still could not stand or walk.
Every time she tried, she tumbled over.

Ms. Lake decided to take Lemon to the vet.

"What your duck has," Dr. Bill explained, "is a balance problem. Not much can be done for this," he said sadly. "You can help her get stronger, but she'll always need extra special care."

When the other three ducks were old enough, they went to live on
Mr. Web's farm. Ms. Lake adopted Lemon and brought her to
school every day. Ms. Lake and her students
did just what the vet ordered — they
gave Lemon extra special care.

Before school each morning, Ms. Lake placed Lemon in a baby stroller and took her for walks around the neighborhood. As the sky loomed above her, Lemon stretched her neck out to get a better look. She watched the birds flitter from tree to tree, or perch on a wire. When Ms. Lake and Lemon got closer to the river, Lemon wagged her tail feathers at the sight of water.

Lemon loved her nightly bath. She strengthened her muscles while she swam in the tub. Her waterproof feathers trapped air like a built-in floatie, and her bones were hollow and light. This made her a natural swimmer.

Ms. Lake often took Lemon to see her feathered siblings at the farm. Peaches, Daisy, and Chip-Chip would waddle over to Lemon and quack a friendly greeting. But they would quickly lose interest in Lemon because she couldn't muck around in the grass (like all ducks love to do).

At school, the children took turns carrying Lemon in a basket. They fed her by hand and gave her oodles of love. Lemon would bark loudly as they left for lunch, and when they returned, she'd quack excitedly as if to say, "Welcome back!"

At recess, Lemon snoozed on the grass as the students surrounded her with treats. Each of the children's bottoms would be in the air as they searched in the grass or under rocks and logs for worms to give to Lemon.

Nathaniel showed the others
how to feed her. "Hold the worm by
Lemon's tail," he'd instruct. "Ms. Lake says Lemon
needs to practice touching her oil gland so she
can get stronger and waterproof herself.
It will keep her dry in the water."

One day, during circle time, Richard asked, "Ms. Lake, how
can we help Lemon stand up?"

"Maybe we can all think of some ideas," she replied.

The next day, Leo brought in balloons from his sister's birthday party. Ms. Lake carefully tied them to each end of a towel and made a sling to hold Lemon up. But Lemon was too heavy, and she popped the balloons with her beak. "How do you get a duck to stand up?" asked Leo.

Day after day, the students tried new ideas, but nothing worked.

Then one weekend, when Holly was helping her parents clean the garage, she spotted the life vest they had once used for their dog when they went on a boat trip.

"Hmm," she thought to herself as she got an idea.

On Monday morning, Holly brought the vest into school and whispered something in Ms. Lake's ear.

Ms. Lake then slid Lemon's legs through the holes of the doggie vest, zipped it up, and grasped the straps as she let the duck's feet touch the floor. Lemon then let out a boisterous "QUACK!"

Everyone stopped what they were doing to see what the noise was all about. "Lemon's standing up!" yelled Myra.

It was true. When the children held the handles of the vest, they could help her stand and walk. When it was time for Lemon to eat, or when she was hanging out at recess or on the rug in the classroom, the vest was attached to a stand so that Lemon could move around on her own.

Lemon was one happy duck. She craned her neck to see everything happening around her. She mucked around in the grass (like all ducks love to do). She was able to find her own worms at recess. She threw out her chest and quacked as if to say, "Look at me!"

Richard's look of happiness turned to one of worry. "Ms. Lake, does this mean Lemon will leave us to go live on Mr. Web's farm?"

"She will stay here, and we will love her and keep her healthy and safe,"
Ms. Lake reassured the students. "Lemon will always need us."

"I think we need her too," Nathaniel said.

Just then, Holly ran up to Ms. Lake and whispered another idea.

The next day at recess, Richard was the first to hear the chorus of quacking. Then the rest of the class heard it too. Mr. Web had brought Peaches, Daisy, and Chip-Chip to school for a visit! The three ducks waddled over to Lemon, who stood proudly in the sling designed by her friends. There the four ducks stood together, looking for treats, and mucking around in the grass (like all ducks love to do).

The students watched, happy to know
that now, their extra special friend
with extra special needs could be part
of both flocks, and they wouldn't
have to say goodbye.

The End